WHERE WAS THE BEAR BORN
WHERE DELIVERED?
BY THE MOON, NEXT TO THE SUN
AMONG THE STARS OF THE PLOUGH
SENT TO EARTH
IN A GOLDEN CRADLE
WITH SILVERY CHAINS.

~ SONG OF THE ~
BIRTH OF THE BEAR

OKSI

This is an Em Querido book
Published by Levine Querido

www.levinequerido.com • info@levinequerido.com
Levine Querido is distributed by Chronicle Books LLC
Story and art copyright © 2021 by Mari Ahokoivu
Translation © 2021 by Silja-Maaria Aronpuro
Originally published in Finland by Asema Kustannus
All rights reserved
Library of Congress Control Number: 2021932073
Paperback ISBN - 978-1-64614-112-8
Printed and bound in China

Published September 2021
First printing

The author would like to thank the following establishments for their support:
FILI / Finnish Literature Exchange
The Finnish Cultural Foundation, The North Ostrobothnia Regional Fund
Arts Promotion Centre Finland, comics and illustration
WSOY Literature foundation

MARI AHOKOIVU

OKSI

LQ

LEVINE QUERIDO

MONTCLAIR · AMSTERDAM · HOBOKEN

PROLOGUE

I

Ooo!

HELLO?

ARE YOU COMING?

WELL?

MOM, MILK PLEASE?

WHAT'S THIS?

ARE YOU COMING?

35

39

AW...

THEY'RE ALL STUPID.

I AM A BEAR! I AM A FIERCE BEAR!

I JUST NEED TO PRACTICE A LITTLE MORE ...

GR

GR!

93

IV

141

165

VII

LITTLE POORLING CAME FROM HEAVENS UNWILLING

EMUU COULD NOT COME TO FETCH HER DAUGHTER

AND THE DAUGHTER WOULD NOT COME HERSELF

EMUU MADE LITTLE POORLING TO HELP FETCH THE DAUGHTER

231

IX

FOREVER AND ALWAYS...

XI

BRMMMM

XII

XIII

shhh
DON'T WORRY,
LITTLE ONE...

there is still one more song to be sung

the song of the old gods and the new ones

So, come

'INTO,

the song

OKSI
GUARDIAN
OF THE FOREST

EPILOGUE

-THE-
 END

· A NOTE ON NAMES ·

EMUU
IN EASTERN Finnish AND Karelian MYTHOLOGY,
THE PROGENITOR OF A SPECIES OF ANIMALS OR PLANTS.

SCAUP
THE WATERBIRD IS A PROMINENT FIGURE IN THE CREATION
MYTH OF THE Finnish NATIONAL EPIC, Kalevala.

MANA
AN OLD WORD FOR *death* IN FINNISH.

OKSI
AN OLD WORD, SOME SAY *maybe*
THE ORIGINAL WORD, FOR ~~bear~~ IN FINNISH.

MARI AHOKOIVU (s. 1984)
is an illustrator
and comic artist
from Finland.

OKSI, HER MAGNUM OPUS, WAS
CALLED "BEAUTIFUL, CLEVER, FUNNY,
VIBRANT, AND FULL OF MAGIC" BY
THE BIGGEST NEWSPAPER IN HER HOME
COUNTRY; WAS SHORTLISTED FOR
THE JARKKO LAINE AWARD; AND
HAS NOW BEEN TRANSLATED INTO ENGLISH
AS THE FIRST GRAPHIC NOVEL ON
THE LEVINE QUERIDO LIST.

Some Notes on This Book's Production

The art for the cover, case, and interiors was created by Mari Ahokoivu using a mix of tradi-
tional (watercolour, ink and a nib pen) and digital tools (Photoshop and Wacom Cintiq drawing
board). The type was hand-lettered throughout by Ahokoivu. The book was printed on FSC™-
certified 120gsm Golden Sun woodfree paper and bound in China.

Production was supervised by Leslie Cohen and Freesia Blizard
Book cover and case designed by Jonathan Yamakami
Book interiors designed by Mari Ahokoivu
Edited by Nick Thomas